THE
FABULOUS

The Hidey Hole

4

Enid Blyton

THE FABULOUS 4

The Hidey Hole

Adapted and Edited by
Jenny Cooke

HarperCollins*Publishers*

HarperCollins*Publishers*
77–85 Fulham Palace Road, London W6 8JB
www.fireandwater.com

First published in Great Britain in 1964
by Lutterworth Press

This edited and adapted edition published in 2000
by HarperCollins*Publishers*

1 3 5 7 9 10 8 6 4 2

Copyright © 2000 Enid Blyton Ltd
Enid Blyton's signature is a trademark of Enid Blyton Ltd

A catalogue record for this book is
available from the British Library

ISBN 0 00 274086 9

Printed and bound in Great Britain by
Omnia Books Limited, Glasgow

Contents

1 Blackberry time   1

2 On the common   7

3 A surprise for John   13

4 Lots of blackberries,
   big as can be   19

5 A lovely job!   27

6 Blackie in trouble   33

7 The hidey hole   39

8 Burglars!   47

9 Down the hidey hole again –
   and a little surprise!   53

10 A thrilling plan   59

11 Oh, what an excitement!   67

12 A very happy ending   75

1

Blackberry time

'Sam! Rosie! Hello! Are you there? Sam! Rosie! Where are you?'

Mummy looked up from her sewing. 'Honestly! It's cousin John again, come to call for Sam and Rosie. Well, he'll just have to wait until they get back home. What a voice he's got! Oh, thank goodness. Here they are.'

Sam and Rosie came in at the back door, each with a carrier of shopping. 'Hello, Mummy. Haven't we been quick? Oh listen! Is that John yelling for us to go round to Whitewalls Cottage again?'

'Yes, it is,' said Mummy, taking the shopping out of the bags. 'He sounds as bad as a foghorn! I've never heard such yells in all my life. For goodness' sake, go over and find out what he wants. I should think he's woken up all the babies in the village by now.'

'SA-AM! RO-SIE!' came John's voice again.

'Oh, I expect he wants to talk to us about going blackberrying,' said Rosie. 'Sarah's ill in bed with flu, so he'll have no one to go with.'

'Do you remember what we told you, Mummy?' asked Sam. 'Our teacher at school said there are so many blackberries this year that we could pick loads and loads and then sell them. We're being sponsored by school to raise as much money as we can for the new Dogs' and Cats' Home in the next village.'

'Yes,' said Rosie. 'There are some sad and lonely dogs and cats and no one wants them. So if they can build a new Home for them, they'll be happy and well fed.' Her eyes filled with tears.

'Oh yes, you did tell me,' said Mummy. 'Now don't cry, Rosie. I'm sure you and Sam will pick lots and lots of blackberries and be able to sell them.'

'Yes, we will!' said Rosie, looking more cheerful again. 'Mummy, will you buy black-berries from us if we pick a lot?'

'Of course, darling,' said Mummy. 'And I'll pay you for any little jobs you do for me. Keep a special box for your earnings. It'll soon be full. I'll make some jam with the blackberries, so pick the very biggest, juiciest ones you can find. Now, *do* go and see what John wants!'

'SAM! ROSIE!' came John's enormous voice again. 'I WANT YOU!' A volley of loud barks followed his shouts, and Mummy put her hands over her ears.

'Honestly! That's Blackie, John's little spaniel puppy, barking his head off now! Do go over and see them, and stop them making all that noise!'

'OK,' said Sam, and he and Rosie ran off at top speed. 'COM-ING!' yelled Sam. 'WE'RE COM-ING!'

Soon the two of them were in John's garden. He was up a tree which overhung the next-door neighbour's garden, and Blackie, his spaniel puppy, was barking his head off just below.

'You've been ages,' said John. 'I've been shouting for you to come over for hours!'

'You haven't!' said Rosie. 'Go on, move up. Make room for us on your branch. Our

3

Mummy was cross with you for shouting so loudly. What do you want anyway? And is Sarah better yet?'

'It's about going blackberrying,' said John, 'and no, Sarah isn't better. She's still in bed.' He slid further up the branch of the old tree to make room for Sam and Rosie. 'Would you two like to come with me after tea? My Mum says you can come to tea first if you like. Then we can go up to the common with Blackie and take the biggest bags we can find. I'll bet we'll pick enough to get more sponsorship money than anyone else!'

'We'll have to pick hundreds and thousands and millions then,' said Rosie, laughing.

'Oh well, we'll just pick as many as we can,' said Sam.

Just then a bell rang in the distance and at once the children slid down the branch and leapt to the ground.

'Tea!' cried John. 'Come on! Mum's made the biggest chocolate-chip buns you've ever seen. You can yell over the road and tell your mother that you're both having tea with us.'

'I think we'd better go and tell her,' said

Sam. 'She gets fed up if she hears us shouting too much.' So while Sam ran off to Corner Cottage to tell his mother, John and Rosie walked up the garden to his house.

'Look at Blackie,' said John, as the puppy scurried up the garden path. 'He runs fast, doesn't he? And he's only a pup!' John was very fond of his puppy, and the little thing adored him. Sam and Rosie thought he was the nicest dog they'd ever seen, and the cleverest.

Soon they were sitting at the tea table. Aunty Eleanor certainly *had* made enormous chocolate-chip buns that afternoon. 'Absolutely stuffed with chocolate chips!' said Rosie. 'I do like your buns, Aunty Eleanor.'

'So does Blackie!' said John's mother, who was keeping a sharp eye on the puppy, watching to see that John didn't slip one or two buns to him under the table. 'Now, John, if you feed Blackie at mealtimes I'll send him straight to his kennel!'

'That was only a crumb I dropped,' said John.

'Is Sarah better yet?' asked Rosie when they'd finished.

'Well,' said Aunty Eleanor, 'she's still feeling rather poorly and when I offered her a chocolate-chip bun, she said her throat hurt too much to swallow it.'

'Oh, the poor thing,' said Sam. 'Perhaps we'd better save her one for tomorrow.'

'Mummy,' said John, 'can we go blackberrying after tea? And can we have some big, strong carriers, please, to put them in? We're going to pick hundreds and hundreds.'

'All right,' said his mother. 'Blackie will love the walk to the common. I'll buy whatever you pick. I know about the sponsorship scheme at school. You can go as soon as you've finished your tea.'

Now there they all go with their carrier bags. Look – even Blackie is carrying a bag in his mouth, just a little one because he's only a puppy. Hurry up, Blackie, or you'll be left behind!'

2

On the common

It was a lovely sunny evening when the three children and Blackie reached the common. They all loved the common. It was glorious in spring when the bluebells and golden gorse were out and the birds were singing madly in the bushes. It was lovely in the summer, when the ferns unfolded their curled-up fingers and the grass was full of tiny, bright flowers. But oh, the joy of autumn! Then the bushes were crowded with big, juicy blackberries. There were always plenty to take home to their mother.

'Blackberries! Blackberries!' sang Rosie, as they came to the common. 'Loads of blackberries, hundreds of blackberries, thousands...'

'*Where* are all those blackberries you're singing about?' asked John, stopping and looking around. 'I can only see a few rather unripe ones on that bush over there.'

'Oh well, there'll be plenty further on,' said Rosie. 'Where's Blackie? I hope he's not gone after a rabbit. Call him, John.'

'Blackie!' yelled John, and the puppy appeared at once from behind a bush with a piece of wood in his mouth. He ran straight to John and dropped the wood at his feet. He wagged his tail hard and gave a little bark as if to say, 'Well, come on now, throw it for me!'

John groaned. 'Oh, honestly, don't say you expect me to throw bits of wood for you all the time, Blackie. I thought you'd grown out of that. Take it away!'

Blackie's tail went down at once, and he looked mournfully round to see if anyone else would throw his bit of wood for him.

'I'll throw it for you, Blackie,' said Rosie and picked it up. She threw it hard, but – oh no! – it went straight into a prickly bush and Blackie gave a mournful howl.

'Just like a girl,' said John in disgust. 'I've never ever seen a girl who could throw anything straight!'

At once Rosie picked up a fallen fir cone from the ground and hurled it straight at John. It hit him on the nose and he yelled. The other two roared with laughter at John's surprise.

'Good shot, Rosie!' cried Sam. John couldn't help grinning as he rubbed his nose. Blackie ran to the fallen fir cone and picked it up in his mouth. He went to Rosie and dropped it at her feet as if to say, 'Do that again!'

'Oh no you don't!' said John promptly, and kicked it away. 'Come on, let's look for blackberries. BLACKIE, STOP PICKING UP FIR CONES! What about finding a bush with blackberries on instead?'

They went on into the bushes, looking for blackberries to put in their empty bags. It was quite incredible how few there were! It was very disappointing. There were hardly any, just one black one here and there.

'You can see where plenty have been *picked*,' said Rosie, looking at a bush where there were many sturdy briar sprays. 'Look at that. There are the bare places where the blackberries grew. Someone must have been here before us. We'd better go further on, where the common's wilder and thicker. I don't think Aunty Eleanor will mind. After all, there are three of us and Blackie as well. We'll be quite safe and we might find some then.'

But all they saw were children like themselves, trying to find a few blackberries to put into their bags and baskets. 'Are you looking for blackberries too?' they asked. 'There just aren't any, are there?'

'Who's had them all, then?' asked Rosie, puzzled. 'There were plenty ripening last time I came here.'

'Look! Can you see that small holiday caravan park over there in that hollow, sheltered by those trees?' said John, pointing. 'It's over there, by that stream. Well, that wasn't here last year. Do you think the children on holiday have picked all the blackberries?'

'Yes, look! There are people with bags and baskets near the caravans,' said Rosie.

'Oh no! We've come too late. All the best blackberries have gone!' John went over to the caravans. They looked rather exciting. What a lot of fun to have a house on wheels and go wherever you liked!

A boy with a sunburnt face called to him. 'You after some blackberries? Well, you're unlucky! I reckon we've picked them all since we've been here. What a huge crop there was. Look at what I picked this morning!'

John looked. The boy's basket was crammed to the top with big, juicy, shining blackberries. They made his mouth water even to look at them! 'You might have left some for us,' he said.

'Well, it's everyone for himself when the blackberries are ripe!' said the boy. 'You should have come sooner. But I tell you what, you can have half of ours.'

'Ooh, thanks!' said John, delighted.

'But only if you pay for them,' added the boy with a cheeky grin.

'Don't be silly!' said John. 'We're going to sell what we picked because our school's sponsoring...'

'Oh yes! A blackberry tart with cream, I suppose!' said the boy. 'Well, first come, first served.' And with that the boy disappeared through the door of the nearest caravan, swinging his full basket. 'Bye!' he called over his shoulder.

'We'll have to go somewhere else and start looking for blackberries,' said John, going back to the others. 'There's none left here. Come on, let's go further on. We've just *got* to find some to sell. We've only picked about ten-pence-worth so far. Come on, everyone!'

3

A surprise for John

It was a very, very disappointing evening. No sooner had they gone a little further on and at last found a few blackberries than it began to pour with rain. 'Oh, I don't believe it!' said Sam, putting up his anorak hood. 'Now we'll have to go back home with only about thirty wet blackberries for our evening's work!'

'If only we'd been able to pick hundreds like that boy did,' said Rosie, almost in tears. 'I was really looking forward to selling whole bags of blackberries and getting a lot of money to give to Miss Allen at school for sponsoring the Dogs' and Cats' Home.'

'I bet all the others will have found plenty,' said John gloomily. 'Miss Allen will think we're a feeble lot. Does anyone know a place where there are usually plenty of blackberries besides on this common?'

'Well, there's Hilltop Common, but that's too far,' said Rosie. 'Too far to go now, anyway. Let's go back home quickly. I'm not going anywhere else this evening. I'm getting soaked!'

It was a rather miserable little group who made their way home as quickly as possible. Rain trickled down their necks and soaked their socks and shoes. They parted company when they came to John's cottage. He and Blackie disappeared through their gate, and Rosie and Sam crossed the road to their own house. What a horrible ending to a lovely plan.

'Well, how many hundreds of blackberries did you pick for me to buy from you?' asked their mother when Sam and Rosie went to find her. 'My goodness! How wet you are!'

'Mummy, we hardly found any blackberries at all,' said Rosie, almost in tears. 'Lots of people must have been to the common before us. We were too late.'

'And we saw a boy from the holiday caravan park who showed us a whole basketful he'd picked,' said Sam. 'I expect the holiday-makers went all round the bushes, picked all they saw and ate them!'

'It was a pity you didn't go sooner,' said Mummy. 'Never mind. Perhaps next time you'll find another place to go blackberrying.'

'But the blackberries will soon be over,' said Rosie. 'And we must get some money for the Dogs' and Cats' Home!'

'Well, you can do some jobs for me,' said Mummy, 'and I'll pay you.'

'But that isn't the same,' said Rosie. 'We don't like you to pay us for doing things for you, Mummy. We like to do them for love. And picking blackberries would have been such fun!'

'Yes, it would,' said Mummy. 'Well, don't get upset. What about a game of Snap? I'm longing to have one!'

'Are you really, Mummy?' said Sam, cheering up. He loved playing Snap. 'Well, if you're sure you'd like a game, I'll get the cards.'

They soon forgot their disappointment over the blackberries, especially as somehow or other Mummy didn't say 'Snap!' as quickly as usual, and the children won easily.

'Very good!' said their mother. 'Here's fifty pence each for the Dogs' and Cats' Home fund, for beating me and winning all my cards.'

'Oh, thank you!' said Sam, and Rosie's eyes shone. One pound was better than nothing. It was a beginning, anyway. Sam slipped the two fifty pence coins into the money box. 'That'll probably buy a brick or two,' he said to Rosie. 'We'll think of something else to do tomorrow, when we see John.'

They went round to John's house the next morning, which was Saturday. 'I don't know where he is,' said Aunty Eleanor. 'He and Blackie have gone off somewhere. I heard Blackie barking at the top of his voice about twenty minutes ago. Maybe he's somewhere in the garden. Could you go and have a look? Sarah's still quite poorly today and I think I'm going to have to send for the doctor,' added Aunty Eleanor in a worried voice. 'Let's hope she gets better soon!'

'Oh yes, we do hope so,' said Sam and Rosie together.

Then the two children went to look for John, but couldn't find him anywhere. How strange! They shouted for him, but there was no answer, so at last they went back to their own garden.

Where *was* John? Well, he was having a little adventure all on his own, right at the very bottom of his garden. He had gone down there to see if he could find a trowel in the garden shed, with Blackie beside him as usual. And then Blackie had begun to bark very loudly indeed and had shot out of the shed and down the path to the hedge at the bottom.

'Blackie! What's up?' yelled John, surprised. 'Be quiet, or you'll wake up Sarah! Oh, BLACKIE! You've seen that ginger cat again. But what's the good of chasing it? You know you can never catch it. COME HERE!'

But Blackie didn't take any notice at all. How dare that ginger cat come into *his* garden? Wuff – wuff – wuff!

The scared cat ran for its life through the hedge at the bottom of the garden, a hedge that divided John's and Sarah's garden from the one beyond, which belonged to a rather fierce and cross old man.

Blackie came to the hedge and squeezed

through it after the cat. John raced after him, shouting. But no Blackie came back. What had happened to the silky-haired, black spaniel puppy? John pictured him being scratched and mauled by that big old ginger cat. How dreadful! John tried to force his way through the thick hedge, and at last managed to get his head through and peer round. No ginger cat – and no Blackie either.

There was something else, though, something that made John stare in wonder and delight. There were great big bramble bushes at the bottom of the next-door garden and they were covered, absolutely covered, in the biggest, finest blackberries he'd ever seen. Nobody had picked them. Perhaps nobody had even seen them. The old man couldn't have wanted them. Oh, what hundreds and thousands there were there, just *waiting* to be picked. What a surprise! What a wonderful surprise!

4

Lots of blackberries,
big as can be

John suddenly remembered Blackie. Had the
puppy attacked the ginger cat, or had the cat
attacked the puppy? He'd better go and find
out. So he cautiously made his way through a
thin place in the hedge, and at last stood in the
other garden, looking all round.

Nobody was there, nobody at all, not
even Blackie. John walked to the blackberry
bushes, which were all tangled up together. He
couldn't help tasting two or three of the
berries. They tasted absolutely fantastic, and
what millions there seemed to be! Were they
all going to be wasted? Dare he go and find
that old man and ask him? People said he had
a very bad temper and had once thrown a
tramp out of his garden, right over the front

hedge. John didn't want to be thrown over *his* garden hedge.

He crept through the blackberry bushes, which tried to catch hold of him with their curved thorns. No Blackie. No ginger cat. No barks, no mews. It was very strange. A pine cone fell from a tall tree nearby and made him jump. His heart began to beat quickly. Then he saw a woman in an apron hanging out some clothes on a washing line in the distance. That would be the old man's home help. She was supposed to be rather a cross person too. Well, John simply had to find out what had happened to his puppy, so up the garden he went, and the home help suddenly saw him.

'Hey! What are you doing? You've come to look for your puppy, I suppose,' she said, looking rather disagreeable. 'Chasing my cat like that! I've locked him up in that shed.'

'The cat's not in there too, is she?' asked John anxiously. 'She might scratch his eyes out.'

'Serve him right too!' said the cross old woman. 'He shouldn't come in here, and no more should you. What do you think you're doing? How dare you come walking up our garden!'

'Er ... for two reasons really,' said poor John, wishing he was back at home. 'One to ask you if you'd like me to pick some of those lovely blackberries for you – the ones at the bottom of your garden. I know the bushes are prickly, and I don't expect you like being scratched by the thorns, but I'd gladly pick you a basketful if you like. I'm sure you haven't time to pick any.'

'What? Blackberries! Who wants blackberries, the nasty, pippy things?' said the home help. 'Not me, and not my employer either. Let them wither away on the bushes; they're not worth the bother of picking! You'd better go and get your dog out of the shed. He's barking loudly now and my employer will be after him if he hears that row!'

John went quickly to the shed and opened the door. Blackie shot out and threw himself madly at his young master, whining in delight.

'Take him away at once!' ordered the woman. 'What a noisy little creature! Don't you let him come near Ginger again. He'll be

21

sorry if he tries it again. Now go home, both of you!'

She went stiffly up the garden with her empty laundry basket, grumbling away to herself. John went quickly in the opposite direction, down to the thick hedge. He looked longingly at the laden blackberry bushes as he passed them. Millions and millions and millions of fat blackberries! He couldn't believe it, all going to waste! Surely it must be wrong to waste them? He really must ask his mother about it.

He set off up the garden with Blackie at his heels, now safely rescued from the shed, and saw his mother picking flowers. She called to him, 'I'm picking some flowers for Sarah to cheer her up. The doctor's been and he thinks she'll soon be on the mend. And John, Sam and Rosie came to see you, but they couldn't find you anywhere. Have you been blackberry hunting or something?'

'No,' said John. 'Mummy, it's quite all right to go and pick blackberries growing anywhere, isn't it?'

'Of course, dear,' said his mother. 'Why do you ask?'

'Well, I was just thinking,' said John. 'I've seen loads and loads of blackberries growing quite wild, and nobody wants them. I know they don't because I asked. They told me the blackberries could wither on the bushes, but *they* weren't going to pick them. Would it be all right if I picked them instead and sold them to help the Dogs' and Cats' Home?'

'Of course,' said his mother, gathering up her flowers. 'It's not right to waste things. I've often told you that. If they're not wanted, then anyone can pick them! Blackie, come off that flowerbed. There are *no* bones buried there!'

John was so delighted to hear his mother say that it wasn't right to let unwanted blackberries go to waste, that he couldn't wait to tell the others. He knew really that he hadn't mentioned that the blackberries were in next door's garden, but he squashed that thought down at once. He went to his front garden and saw Sam and Rosie across the road, digging in their sandpit. He called to them, 'Sam! Rosie! Come over here quickly. I've got a secret!'

Sam flung down his spade and he and Rosie crossed the road carefully and then raced up

John's front drive. A secret! This was exciting.

'Listen,' said John in a whisper. 'I've found bushes of blackberries, bushes and bushes, covered with the biggest blackberries you've ever seen. Nobody wants them. They're going to waste. We could get baskets full to the top!'

'Where?' asked Sam and Rosie, amazed.

'Come and see,' said John, and took them down to the bottom of the garden. He made them look through a space in the hedge, and they saw the great blackberry bushes. 'My mother said it would be quite all right to pick them, as nobody wants them,' he said. 'What do you think of that? We could pick kilos and kilos of them!'

Sam and Rosie were so astonished at the wonderful sight they saw through the hedge, that at first they couldn't say a word. Then Rosie caught hold of John's arm, her eyes shining brightly.

'We'll pick some now, this very minute! We'll sell them to Mummy, and give Miss Allen the money towards the Dogs' and Cats' Home.'

'And tomorrow we'll pick some more and the next day, after school, some more still!'

said Sam, red with excitement. 'It's like magic, seeing all those great big blackberries waiting to be picked! Did Aunty Eleanor really say it would be all right to pick them? Wow! What fun we're going to have!'

'Wuff!' barked Blackie joyfully, joining in the excitement. 'Wuff!'

Then Rosie suddenly burst into a funny little song that came into her head:

Hooray for blackberries, big as can be,
Hooray for blackberries, lots for you
*   and me,*
Hooray for dogs and cats, for very soon
*   they'll see,*
A lovely new Home, as smart as can be!

Yes, three cheers, Rosie. That's wonderful! You'd better start picking blackberries straight-away. Honestly, what a lot there are!

5

A lovely job!

The three children and Blackie raced up to John's house. 'I know where there are some baskets, in the hall cupboard,' said Rosie. And sure enough, there they were: one very big one, two middle-sized ones, and a small one. The children took them all except the very big one. 'It would take days to fill that!' said Rosie. 'I like a basket I can fill quickly. Oh, what an amazing find, John! All those bushes, stuffed to bursting with blackberries. There are such a lot, we can eat as many as we like and *still* fill our baskets to the brim!'

'Wuff!' said Blackie, dancing round excitedly. He didn't know what the excitement was all about, but he was quite determined to join in.

'Oh Blackie, you're lovely,' said Sam happily. 'It's a pity you can't pick blackberries too. Just be careful you don't upset our baskets when they're full, or you'll get into trouble!'

'Wherever are you all going?' asked John's mother, hearing all the commotion in the hall and coming to see what it was all about.

'To pick blackberries!' shouted John as he ran out of the door.

'Hundreds of them!' called Rosie.

'I'll buy them from you!' replied Aunty Eleanor. 'You can have them stewed with sugar and yoghurt.'

But nobody heard her. They were halfway down the garden, longing to get at those wonderful blackberry bushes!

They squeezed through the hedge and went over to the bushes. Now they were so close to them, they were even more amazed. What a fantastic crop of blackberries! How incredible that the old man and his home help didn't want them.

'The home help with the washing called them "nasty, pippy things"!' said John, popping a big juicy berry into his mouth and biting it so that the sweet juice ran all over his tongue. 'Ooh! That was the best blackberry I've ever tasted. I must have a few more!'

'Well, don't forget to pick some for us, greedy!' said Rosie. 'Hey! Look at this one. It's a giant!'

'I think we ought to line our baskets with some big leaves,' said Sam, looking down at his basket. 'The blackberries are so ripe, they're a bit squishy and they'll make the baskets messy. Look, let's pick some leaves off that big tree and line our baskets with them.'

'That's a good idea,' said Rosie, and they all picked the smooth leaves from the nearby tree and neatly lined the bottoms of their baskets.

It was great fun picking the black, juicy fruit. Soon their fingers were stained and their mouths were as purple as the berries. The sun shone down hotly and Blackie began to pant. He lay down under a bush, looking up at the children as if to say, 'Go on picking, but don't expect me to help!'

'My basket's half-full already,' said Rosie, pleased. 'It's a pity today's Saturday and not

Monday. I'd have loved to take these baskets to school to show the others how many we'd picked!'

'I'll bet nobody will find as many berries as we shall,' said Sam. 'I wish I'd brought that very big basket now. I bet I could have filled it to the brim. Do you suppose that would be two whole pounds' worth?'

'Oh, yes, easily,' said Rosie. 'Blackberries are always very expensive in the shops.'

'Listen – I can hear voices!' said John suddenly. 'Someone's coming down the garden. I hope it isn't that cross old man. He might just be annoyed with us.'

They hid behind the tallest bush and Rosie peered through the leaves. 'It's all right,' she said. 'He's stopped to smell a rose or something. He's in a wheelchair that he can manage himself. He does look a bit fierce.'

'He's supposed to be very, very rich,' said Sam. 'And I overheard my mother say that his house is full of beautiful things.'

'Worth hundreds and hundreds of pounds,' said Rosie. 'I'd be afraid of burglars, wouldn't you, John?'

'No, because I've always got Blackie around,' said John. 'He'd frighten away at least ten burglars, wouldn't you, Blackie?'

'Wuff!' said Blackie at once in a very loud bark, and then he growled fiercely.

'Sh! The old man will hear you,' said John. 'Oh! He *has* heard you! Quick, get back through the hedge everyone. Blow! I've spilt my blackberries!'

A loud voice came to their ears. 'Is anyone there? Who's that down in my garden?'

The children felt frightened. Suppose the old man didn't want them to pick blackberries? Perhaps he liked to let them go to waste each year? Oh, it wasn't fair. He might tell their parents and get them into trouble. Sam and Rosie fled to the hedge at once, but John stayed with Blackie, hoping to have time to pick up his spilt berries.

Then, oh no! Who should come walking along, tail held straight up in the air, but the big ginger cat! Of course, Blackie saw her at once. He gave a great bark and the cat fled up a tree. John caught hold of Blackie's collar before he could chase the cat, and dragged him down to the hedge.

'Who's there? What's happening?' shouted the old man, but there was no answer. John was almost through the hedge, hanging onto Blackie's collar for all he was worth. But what a shame: he'd left all his precious spilt blackberries behind!

6

Blackie in trouble

Rosie and Sam went to help Blackie out of the hedge. He was caught by a prickly branch. Rosie was frightened. 'I shan't go blackberrying there again,' she said. 'I'm scared of that old man. He's got such a loud, cross voice. Oh, John, where's your basket of blackberries?'

'I spilt them all,' said John gloomily. 'I'll go back and pick them up when I think it's safe. I left the basket there too. I hope the old man doesn't find it. He might keep it and then my mother would want to know where it had gone.'

'He might still be watching out to see if we go back again,' said Sam. 'I do hope it doesn't matter picking his blackberries.'

'Well, I told you my mother said if they were

growing wild, and nobody wanted them, we could pick them,' said John.

'Yes, but you didn't tell her they were in someone else's *garden*,' said Sam.

'All right. All right. I just wanted to get as much money as we could for the Dogs' and Cats' Home,' said John. 'And if all those berries were going to waste, why shouldn't we have them?'

'If there's no reason why we shouldn't have them, why didn't you go and ask the old man if we could pick them?' asked Rosie.

'I'm not going to answer your stupid questions!' said John crossly. 'Are you going to sell your blackberries?'

'Yes. I expect Mummy will buy them,' said Sam. 'And we'll take the money to Miss Allen on Monday. What about *your* blackberries? Are you going to pick them up and put them in your basket and take them to Aunty Eleanor? You'd better get them quickly, though. They're very ripe and they'll soon go bad, unless you get them into the fridge quickly!'

That was an awful thought. All that work of picking for nothing. John frowned. 'I'll go and pick up all my spilt blackberries, put them back in my basket, and pick lots more too! Then I'm going to sell them for *much* more money than either of you two will!' he said, his nose in the air. 'I'll bet my mother will pay me more for my blackberries than Aunty Sue will for yours!'

'I'll bet she won't!' said Sam at once. 'Anyway, we're going to take them to our mother now and ask her if she'd like them. We'll leave you to pick yours up. Hope they won't all be spoilt!'

Sam and Rosie went off with their baskets of blackberries. John scowled after them. He didn't fancy the crawl back through the hedge to pick up his spilt blackberries one little bit. That old man might be on the watch. Yet it would be a shame to waste all those lovely berries. He peered through the hedge. The cat seemed to have gone. There was no sign of the old man either.

'I could slip back now and pick up my blackberries,' thought John. 'The cat's gone. The old man's disappeared, and the home help isn't anywhere about. Yes, I'll slip through the hedge now.'

So he crawled through the hedge once again, and soon found himself on the other side. Everything was quiet. The leaves rustled a little, but that was a nice noise. There came a whine behind him and John frowned.

'Blackie! I didn't want you to come. That ginger cat may be prowling about somewhere, and you'll only go after it. Go back home!'

But Blackie sat himself down firmly and stared at John. John knew what that meant. Blackie wasn't going to do anything he didn't want to do!

'All right then! Just sit there and keep quiet,' said John crossly. 'I'm going to pick up my blackberries, and I don't want any help from you, see? You can give a little growl if you hear anyone coming, but that's all. No whines and no barks. Sit!'

Blackie sat without moving. Even his tail was quite still. He stared hard at John as if to say, 'Hurry up, I'm getting tired of all this!'

Then the ginger cat came stalking up again. John didn't see it; he was too busy picking up his spilt blackberries. But Blackie saw it at once and gave a furious growl. *That cat again*

– *grrrr*! The cat was very rude. She spat at Blackie and then fled under a bush. Blackie was shocked. He wasn't used to being spat at. He leapt after the ginger cat, barking loudly, and made poor John almost jump out of his skin. The boy dropped all his blackberries again as he made a grab for Blackie's collar.

'Be quiet!' said John as loudly as he dared. But Blackie slipped away from him and disappeared under a great blackberry bush. There was a scrabbling noise inside the bush, and then a whine. The cat fled up the garden.

'Blackie, where are you?' said John anxiously in a low voice. 'Are you hurt? Where've you gone, Blackie? I can't see you. Oh, I don't believe it. You haven't broken a leg or anything, have you? Blackie!'

A miserable little whine came from somewhere. 'Oh Blackie, I can't see where you are!' wailed John. 'These bushes are so thick and prickly. Come out at once, you daft dog!'

There came some more whines, but no Blackie appeared. John felt scared. He crawled further under the great bush and peered about. Another whine came, quite near now.

'Oh Blackie! You're down a hole! Honestly, where on earth are you? There's a sort of cave under this big bush. You've fallen into it! Let me get hold of your collar and I'll try and pull you out. Oh dear, dear Blackie, you *are* hurt. I know you are! Wait till I can get down beside you and I'll help you out. Here I come! I'm on my way now.'

7

The hidey hole

John felt the blackberry bush prickles catching hold of him as he forced his way under the thick bush to poor Blackie. The puppy was very frightened and was whining pitifully. Only his head could be seen.

'You're in some kind of very peculiar hole,' said John, puzzled, as he reached the dog at last. 'Hey! Don't struggle so much, or you'll sink further down into the hole if you do. There now, you've slipped again. Let me get in beside you and I'll soon push you out.'

But the hole was a much bigger one than John had imagined it to be. In fact, it was a very odd hole indeed. It was quite deep and quite wide, and the sides were hard, as if they'd been flattened by a spade.

'It doesn't look like an old rubbish pit somehow,' said John, putting his arm round Blackie. 'Though it might have been before these enormous bushes grew over it. Where's my little torch gone? It's really dark down here; the bushes are so thick! Let me see if you're hurt, Blackie.'

He took his torch from his pocket and switched it on. He examined the puppy. 'You've got a nasty scratch on your nose. Done by one of those rotten thorns, I suppose,' said John. 'And I think you've hurt your back leg, though it may only be bruised. Poor, poor little Blackie. This really is a bigger hole than I thought. What *can* this have been used for, before the bushes grew over it? I'll bet it was a sort of hidey hole. But what did it hide? Escaped prisoners? Hidden money? Or what?'

He swung his torch all around. He saw a neat little hole by his head and put his hand into it. Something was there – a little chain with four keys on it. How very strange! And here was another hole, further down. It was a bigger one. John put his hand into that one too, and felt something hard. He pulled it out and shone his torch onto it. 'A cup! Well, well! Somebody's been down here at some time and used this hole under the bushes as a hidey hole. But why? Blackie, we'll have a really good look, shall we, and see what else we can find.'

Two more holes were discovered by John's torch. An old newspaper was in one, all crumpled up. John put it carefully into one of his pockets. In the other hole was a knife with a very sharp blade indeed. John looked at it and frowned. 'Who is it who hides down here, perhaps sleeps down here, and why? I don't like it, Blackie, and I'm quite glad you're with me. I wouldn't like to be found by the owner, whoever he is, unless I had you with me! I wonder if the cross old man knows anything about this hidey hole? He couldn't have put these things down here, could he?'

Blackie gave a tired little whine. He didn't like this hole. He was tired. He wanted to be in his comfortable dog basket, away from cats and prickly bushes. John put his arm round him. 'All right, we'll go back now. I think it'll be quite safe. That ginger cat will have got tired of waiting about for you. Come on, let's go. It's a bit stuffy down here. What an exciting thing to tell Sam and Rosie – a big hidey hole under the bushes. And Sarah can come and have a look when she's better. What a pity it isn't in our garden, Blackie. We could play smugglers as much as we liked. We might even make a passage from the hole all the way up the garden!'

'Wuff,' said Blackie rather dismally. He didn't want to have anything more to do with holes. He just wanted to go back home!

'Now we must be careful,' whispered John, as he began to force his way upwards. 'Nobody must see us or hear us. This is a very, very secret hidey hole, and it's ours now, Blackie. I've always wanted a hidey hole, haven't you? One that nobody else knew about. You're not to tell anyone about it at all, not even the dog across the road! We don't want him coming here to hide his smelly old bones!'

The two of them heaved and scraped their way out of the strange hole, and then crawled under the thick blackberry bushes. At last they were in the open air once more. What a mess John looked, his clothes torn, his face scratched and his hair standing up on end. Blackie hardly knew him!

'Wow!' said John, looking down at himself. 'I'd better clean myself up a bit before Mum sees me looking like this! You look a bit peculiar too, Blackie. You're covered in bits and pieces.'

They both looked very peculiar. John brushed himself down as well as he could, and picked some of the biggest pieces of earth off his clothes. Then he remembered his spilt blackberries. Yes, they were still there on the ground. Good! The basket was still there too. He had just begun to pick up the blackberries when he thought he heard a noise. He ran to hide, but a cheerful voice called to him: 'John! Where on earth have you been? We've been looking everywhere for you. Honestly, I've never seen anyone looking such a mess!'

It was Sam, peering through the hedge. He scrabbled right through and began to help John pick up the spilt blackberries. 'My mother gave me fifty pence for my blackberries,' he said. 'It's a shame you've spilt yours. Some of them are a bit messy too.'

'Sam,' began John solemnly, 'I've got news for you. Exciting news. I've discovered a—'

'Sam! Where are you? Mummy says come at once because Aunty Eleanor's here!' someone cried from the other side of the hedge. It was Rosie. 'Oh, do hurry up. I've been looking for you everywhere! SAM!'

'I'm telling Sam something. Something secret and important,' said John crossly. 'I've discovered a hidey hole, a very, very curious hidey hole. It's right under the blackberry bushes. It's really rather mysterious, and—'

'It'll have to wait till tomorrow!' said Rosie. 'I'll bet it isn't much of a hole, anyway. Sam, do come on!'

Sam went off with Rosie. John was very disappointed. He'd so very much wanted to talk about the hidey hole he had found. They could have such fun in it. They could make shelves in it and put their books there. They could have a cardboard box to store food. They could sit down there on wet days, perfectly dry, and nobody in the world would know where they were. And now there was no one to tell. He picked up Blackie and hugged him. 'It's *our* hidey hole, Blackie, yours and mine,' he said. 'And if the others don't want to hear about it, all right, we won't tell them, see!'

'Wuff! Wuff! Wuff!' said Blackie, quite agreeing and wagging his little tail as fast as he could.

'Right. Now we'll finish picking up the blackberries and take them to Mum,' said John. 'But don't say a word to her about the hidey hole, will you, Blackie? NOT ONE SINGLE WORD!'

8

Burglars!

John took his blackberries inside to give to his mother. They had been lying on the grass for some time and didn't look as nice and fresh as they had when they were first picked.

'You could have picked better ones than these, surely, John,' said his mother, who had just got back from Sam's and Rosie's house. 'These are really squashed. I'll give you thirty pence for them, and if you pick me some better ones, I'll make it fifty.'

'I feel a bit tired, Mum,' said John. 'I've had such an exciting time. I'll pick you lots more tomorrow.'

'Where have you been to get so tired?' asked his mother. 'I heard Sam and Rosie calling for you.'

'I've been down at the end of the garden, Mum, and over the hedge,' said John. He didn't say anything about his hidey hole. That was his very own secret.

'Would you like to go down to the supermarket for me and get me some butter?' asked his mother. 'That will earn you another thirty pence to take to Miss Allen. Or are you too tired?'

'Oh, the supermarket isn't far,' said John, cheering up. 'I've *got* to take something to school for Miss Allen's Dogs' and Cats' Home fund, haven't I?'

'Yes, you must,' said his mother. 'I know how much you want to help.'

'I'll go for the butter now. Come here, Blackie. I'll put you on the lead. I'm not going to have you scampering across the busy roads. And just you remember this, when I say HEEL, you come and walk just behind me. This is my HEEL, just here, see?'

'Wuff!' said Blackie, and gave John's heel a loving lick. Then he trotted off with him, waving his tail proudly.

Quite a lot of the schoolchildren were busy that weekend. Many of them picked blackberries to sell to Miss Allen or to the shops. Some went shopping in the village. Some helped their fathers in the garden. Two girls cleaned out the garden shed for their father, and one boy cleaned his mother's bicycle. There was a fine amount of money being saved up for the Dogs' and Cats' Home.

John saw hardly anything of Sam and Rosie. How he longed to take them down to his hidey hole! But before the weekend was over, there was another excitement for everyone.

'Have you heard about the robbery?' called Sam across the road to John. 'That cross old man at the end of the garden had *burglars* last night! Isn't that amazing? Did your Blackie bark?'

'Well, no, he didn't,' said John. 'The end of our garden is rather far away, and the old man's house is further away still, right at the top of his garden. You couldn't expect Blackie to hear anything really.'

'One burglar has been caught already!' shouted Rosie. 'But the second one escaped.'

'What did they steal?' asked John, who was now listening eagerly.

Sam and Rosie crossed over the road and came into John's garden. 'Lovely things,' said Sam. 'A pair of big, real silver goblets, a very old sword that belonged to the old man's father, a gold clock that chimes, some silver candlesticks and ... oh, lots more things. The police couldn't find any of them in the old man's house. And there's an *enormous* reward being offered for all the stolen things. Oh, I *wish* I could find them and win the reward. I'd buy a bicycle and a—'

'People are saying that the robbers hid the things somewhere in Whispering Wood,' said Rosie, trying to get a word in. 'They were seen there yesterday. Sam and I are going to hunt about in the wood. Wouldn't it be incredible if we won the reward?'

'I think I'll come and hunt there too,' said John. 'I know where there are quite a lot of hollow trees. That's the kind of place robbers use for hiding things.'

'Brilliant idea!' said Rosie. 'We'll all go together, shall we? You and me and Sam. We'll have a great time!'

So that afternoon the three of them met

together near Whispering Wood. No, four of them, because Blackie was there too, his tail wagging as fast as it could. He was very proud to be with the children and to go on a robber-hunt. His tail wagged without stopping, and he pranced ahead as if he were the leader of the little party.

'There's a hollow tree over there. The hole is halfway up the trunk,' said John. 'I'll shin up, if you'll help me Sam.'

There was nothing but an old bird's nest in the tree. It was very disappointing. And there was nothing at all in the next hollow tree that John led them to, not even a nest.

After that he forgot where the other hollow trees were, and they all wasted a lot of time looking for holes that weren't there! Blackie hunted about too, but his holes were rabbit holes. He went so far down one hole that the children were really scared that he was lost down there for ever. But he scrabbled back at last, coming out tail first because there wasn't room for him to turn. He was astonished and very pleased at the way the children fussed over him when at last he appeared.

'Oh, Blackie, I thought you'd gone right down to the middle of the earth!' said Rosie, almost in tears. 'Please don't disappear like that again. John, I'm tired of looking for stolen things. Let's go home for tea.'

So off they went, disappointed that they hadn't been able to find the stolen goods and win the prize. Perhaps Blackie knew best: perhaps they were down a rabbit hole!

9

Down the hidey hole again – and a little surprise!

John hadn't said a single word to anyone about his hidey hole, but he talked quite a lot about it to Blackie. Blackie was a lovely dog to talk to because he sat absolutely still, head on one side, and listened very carefully.

'It can be our own little private home, Blackie,' said John. 'We'll go down there if ever anything horrible happens, or when Daddy's cross with us sometimes. We could go and slide down into that hidey hole and stay there until any trouble was over. Blackie, I'll take down a bone or two for you, and maybe some biscuits and peppermints and a bar of chocolate for me. Too bad, the others won't know what they're missing! It'll serve them right for being in too much of a hurry to listen to the most exciting news I've ever had!'

'Wuff,' said Blackie, and cuddled as near to John as he could. He loved John with all his doggy heart and he thought that a hidey hole for biscuits was a very good idea indeed.

It took John a day or two to save up some biscuits. He bought a bottle of lemonade, too, to take down to the hidey hole. 'There's a cup already there,' he told the listening puppy. 'I've no idea who it belongs to, but perhaps it belonged to some boy or girl who lived in the old man's house before he came, and who found the hidey hole just like I did. Now don't you dare tell any of your doggy friends about our hidey hole!'

Rosie and Sam were cross with John because he wouldn't say a single word to them about his secret. 'No. You wouldn't listen when I wanted to tell you, and now I shan't tell you!' he said. 'It's my secret and Blackie's, the most exciting secret we've ever had.'

'Well, we know it's a hidey hole somewhere,' said Sam. 'I bet we'll find it, Rosie and I.'

'I bet you won't!' said John. So he made up his mind to take the biscuits and the lemonade down to the hidey hole that evening. Rosie and Sam wouldn't be about then.

After tea he and Blackie went down to the hedge at the bottom of the garden, John carrying the biscuits and the lemonade, and Blackie carrying in his mouth a small bag of his own biscuits. He felt most important. They squeezed through the hedge and went through the great big blackberry bushes. 'Now, don't make a sound, Blackie,' whispered John. 'You know the way, don't you? Under that bush just there. Quiet now!'

Soon they had both slipped down into the big, dark hidey hole, and John switched on the little torch he always had in his pocket. Oh no! What was this big sheet of paper doing, lying on the floor of the hole? He read it quickly. In big letters was written: '**Ha, ha! We found your hidey hole! Thanks for showing us where it was! We hid and watched you creeping in! We'd like to share it with you! From Sam and Rosie.**'

John tore up the piece of paper, feeling cross. Then he grinned. 'Oh well, Blackie, if they know where our hidey hole is, they might as well share it. It's silly to quarrel, isn't it? Come on, let's go and find them. Hey! What's this in the corner, Blackie? A pencil – look – a silver one, too. Sam must have dropped it. I know he's got one.'

John picked up the neat little pencil and slipped it into his pocket. Then he and Blackie made their way out of the hidey hole, crawled under the prickly bushes and were soon through the hedge and into their own garden again.

John ran into his front garden and looked out for Sam and Rosie. He could hear them playing in their own garden. He called across the road to them. 'Hey! You've been down my hidey hole! What do you think of it?'

Sam and Rosie crossed the road carefully, glad that John wasn't cross. 'It's fantastic!' said Sam. 'Big as anything. Let's play smugglers down there, shall we?'

'Yes, and take lots to eat and drink and have underground picnics,' said Rosie. 'John, who do you think used that hole? Children who came to stay at the house where the old man lives? There are no children who ever come there now.'

'Well, I never thought of that,' said John, frowning. 'Yes, I expect that's who used it. Children like us. They've left a cup there, and a knife and a newspaper. I've got them all. Honestly, I hope the hole doesn't still belong to them. Perhaps they're the grandchildren of that cross old man, and come to stay with him sometimes.'

'We could easily find out,' said Sam.

'Sam, I think you dropped something in the hole when you were down there,' said John, scrabbling in his pocket for the little pencil he'd found. 'Your silver pencil, look. It's really careless of you to lose a lovely thing like that.'

'It's not mine!' said Sam, examining it. 'Mine's here in my pocket, and it's a bit bigger than the one you found.'

'Well! Who's been down the hidey hole besides you two and Blackie and me?' asked John, amazed. 'This pencil wasn't there the last time I was there, I'm sure of that. I'd have seen it. You're sure it's not yours, Sam?'

'No. Here's mine, look. And anyway, the one you found has initials on it that aren't mine. See: P. L. M. Well, P. might stand for

Peter, or Paul, or Patrick, but it doesn't stand for Sam! This belongs to somebody who knows the hidey hole and uses it, John.'

'But ... but WHO would use a hidey hole like that at the bottom of someone's garden, hidden under big bushes?' asked Rosie, amazed. 'And what for? It's a mystery, and do you know what? We're going to solve it! Who uses that hidey hole, and why, and when! Wow! This is exciting, isn't it?'

10

A thrilling plan

The three children were very thrilled about their plan. They decided to visit the hidey hole and talk about it there. Soon they were all down the hole, lit rather dimly by John's torch.

'We won't tell anyone!' said Rosie. 'This is our own secret, our own mystery, and I think we ought to try and find out everything by ourselves.'

'It's a shame we can't tell Sarah about it,' said John, 'but Mum says although she's a bit better she can't come downstairs yet.'

'Well,' said Rosie, 'perhaps she'll be able to come down in a day or two. We can save her some of the chocolate. But apart from Sarah, we won't tell *anyone*!'

'How can we find out who sits down here in this dark hidey hole and writes with a silver pencil?' asked John. 'I shouldn't think it'll be that cross old home help. She may be cross, but she always looks very clean and tidy. I can't see her getting down into this dirty, dark hole!'

'Well, nobody else lives at the house apart from the old man,' said Rosie. 'Anyway, it's got to be somebody who knows there's a hidey hole under the bushes, and I shouldn't think many people know about that! Nobody could possibly guess there's a great big hidey hole here unless he's scrabbled underneath, like we did, and found it. And honestly, nobody but children would do that. Grown-ups would be far too careful about their clothes to crawl down here.'

'Do you think it's a boy or girl who's been hiding for some reason? Perhaps someone who's run away from home? Or perhaps a tramp who wanted shelter last night and left his pencil behind?' said John.

'Why don't we bring our torches and come down here ourselves tonight, when it's dark, and see if there's anyone in our hidey hole then?' said Rosie. 'If they had a torch switched on, we'd see the light and challenge them!'

This all sounded very exciting. Blackie gave a little bark as if to say, 'Good idea! I'll come too!'

'Well, let's arrange to do that then,' said John. 'Can you two creep out without anyone seeing you? I can easily, and anyway I usually take Blackie for a run before I go to bed. If there's any news to report, I'll come over and tell you.'

'Right!' said Sam. 'This is quite an adventure, this hidey hole! Let's have something to eat, shall we? We've got some sweets, look, and a bar of chocolate. We'll share it all out. Adventures make you hungry, don't they?'

'I've got some lemonade and biscuits and some toffees somewhere,' said John, taking a whole mess of things out of his pocket. He picked a sticky bag of toffee from the mess. Blackie sat up at once and begged. 'No, Blackie! You know very well what happens when you have toffee,' said John, handing the others one each.

'What happens?' asked Sam.

'Oh, his teeth get stuck together and that frightens him, and he tears round and round trying to open his mouth and he can't,' said John. 'He nearly goes mad and so does Mum, when he acts like that. So we don't give him toffees any more, but he'd like a bit of chocolate, I'm sure.'

So Blackie had a piece of Sam's chocolate and swallowed it almost whole. 'What a waste!' said John. 'I don't believe he could even have tasted that. Now, what are our plans?'

'Do let's creep through the hedge tonight when it's dark and see if there's a light shining from the hidey hole!' said Rosie.

'What shall we do if there is?' asked John.

'I don't know. Peep and see who's there, and then run for our lives!' said Rosie with a giggle. 'We'll have Blackie with us, won't we? He'll scare whoever's there. Anyway, do let's come and have a look. Though I expect the hole will be dark and empty, except for a few worms and a spider or two!'

'All right. We'll creep through the hedge tonight and have a peep,' said John. 'I'll bet we'll be scared if we do see a light shining out from under the bushes!'

'Is that lemonade in that bottle beside you, John?' said Sam. 'Let's have some, shall we? I'm really thirsty. And did you say something about biscuits?'

'Yes, they're in that hole just behind your head,' said John. 'Hand them out, will you? There's a cup in another hole we can use for lemonade. I'd love to know who uses those holes. I found that silver pencil on the floor, though, so someone must have dropped it and never noticed.'

Soon they were eating biscuits and drinking lemonade. Everything tasted delicious and it felt very exciting to be sitting in such a wonderful hidey hole where nobody, but *nobody* could see them!

'It's getting a bit late,' said John at last. 'I think we'd better go now, in case our mothers start yelling for us. Now listen, it'll be easy for me to slip out, as I said, because I always take Blackie out for a run before I go to bed. I'll be out here about half past seven, OK? Will that be all right for you?'

'Yes, we'll manage that,' said Sam. 'Or I will anyway. Rosie sometimes has to have her bath early, and if so, I'll have to come on my own because she'll have her night things on.'

'Oh, I do hope Mummy doesn't send me for an early bath tonight!' said Rosie.

'Well,' said Sam, 'you'd better wait and see. Now, John, how will I know you're ready for us? Can you hoot like an owl?'

'Yes,' said John, and he gave a wonderful imitation of an owl hooting. 'When you hear that noise, come and join me. Very quietly, though.'

'Right,' said Sam, thrilled to think of going out at night into John's garden in response to the hoot of an owl. 'Come on, Rosie, we really must go. See you later, John. Let's hope we have an adventure!'

Oh, you'll have an adventure all right, Sam! No doubt about that! Hurry back home now with Rosie, though. There's hot toast waiting for you, and strawberry jam, and your mother is getting worried.

Rosie and Sam went through the hedge, across the road, back into their own garden, and raced up to their house. John squeezed through into his garden with Blackie sniffing at his heels. He couldn't help feeling excited. Suppose he did see a light in that hidey-hole? Whatever would he do then?

11

Oh, what an excitement!

John felt very excited after he'd had his tea. If only it would hurry up and get dark! He was so longing to go down and see if anyone was in their hidey hole. Blackie sensed his excitement, and kept whining and pawing at John as if to say, 'Do let's get on with our adventure!'

'You'd better take Blackie out for a run, John,' said his mother at last, and John jumped up at once.

'OK, Mum,' he said, and tore out of the room with Blackie at his heels. Then John caught hold of Blackie's collar. 'Now, listen, no more barks or whines. Sh! I'm going to hoot like an owl, to tell Sam and Rosie we're waiting for them.'

Blackie was quiet at once. John put his two half-closed hands up to his mouth and drew in a deep breath. Then, making a loud 'Ooooooooh' sound in his throat, he blew as hard as he could into his hands. A loud and lovely hoot came from them. 'Oooooooh – oooh – oooh – OOOOOOH!'

It was so like an owl's hoot that Blackie looked round to see if he could see the owl. John waited half a minute and then hooted again. 'Ooooooooh! Oooh – oooh – OOOOH!'

The two children across the road were listening out for the hooting, and as soon as they heard it they went quietly to the back door and slipped out into the half-dark. Across the road they went and down into John's garden, then down to the bottom to join John. Blackie gave a small whine of welcome.

'Hi!' whispered John. 'You weren't long in coming. We'll get through the hedge into the old man's garden now, but honestly, don't make any noise just in case somebody *is* in the hidey hole.'

So, very quietly, the four of them crept through the hedge and went over to the big, shadowy blackberry bushes. Blackie gave a very, very small growl. John stopped at once. What had Blackie heard? He went a step or two further, and then his heart began to beat fast. There was a light shining dimly under the bush where the hidey hole was. Yes, there really was!

There was a quiet voice, too, talking down in the hole. Then came a scrabbling noise as somebody tried to climb out of the hole. It was a man with a torch under one arm and a mobile phone held to his ear. John crouched down behind his bush, hardly daring to breathe. The others kept absolutely still as well. The man was crawling out now from the hidey hole under the big, prickly bushes, his torch still on. He hissed into the phone, 'I'm on my way back now, straight up the garden and away!' And he vanished very quickly indeed up the old man's garden, hardly making a sound!

As soon as he was safely gone, the three children, with Blackie at their heels, went right up to the hidey hole. 'Let's wait for a minute,' whispered John, 'and make sure that man's really gone.'

They crouched down, waiting, listening to their fast-beating hearts. John spoke again, in a low voice, 'I think it's all right now. He must have gone right up the old man's garden and out by the back way.'

'Whatever was he doing down in our hidey hole?' said Sam, half frightened and half thrilled.

'That's what we'll find out,' said John. 'Blackie, stay here and guard us while we're down the hole. Come on you two!'

By the light of John's torch they all slithered down into the hole. John shone his torch round as soon as they were safely there. 'Wow! Look at that!' he said, as the light of his torch gleamed brightly on something in the corner. 'And that!'

'*Candlesticks*! Silver candlesticks! And look at this great old sword! And what are those cup things? How they shine!'

'Silver goblets,' said Rosie, picking one up and nearly dropping it. 'Gosh! It's heavy!'

Ding-dong, ding-dong, ding-dong, ding-dong! What on earth was making that noise?

'It's that golden clock over there. Do you

remember a chiming clock was stolen too?' said John, picking it up. 'Isn't it beautiful. Whatever do we do now?'

'We'll take everything back home, sword and all,' said Sam, 'in case that man comes back for anything. As soon as he and his accomplices find anyone who wants to buy these things, they'll be back like a shot.'

'It must have been them who dropped the silver pencil I found, of course,' said John. 'And hid that cup and that newspaper. They must have used this hole as a hiding place for themselves while they waited for a chance to slip up into the old man's house and take what they wanted.'

'They must have hidden all these things at the back of the hidey hole the other day,' said Sam. 'Somewhere in the shadows, with an old sack over them. And because our torch is so dim, we didn't notice all these things before.'

'Let's not stay here any longer,' said Rosie. 'That man might come back and he might not be on his own next time! Let's carry everything back to our house, or your house, John.'

'We can't possibly carry everything,' said

John. He lifted up an old cloth lying on the ground. 'Look, there's more things here. Silver forks and spoons and—'

'We *can* take everything between us!' said Sam, picking up the two goblets. 'Come on. We'll go to our house. My parents are at home. They'll know exactly what to do.'

So off went the four of them, carrying the stolen goods between them. What a weight they were. And how astounded Sam's parents were when the children came staggering in with such a load! They leapt up from their chairs in amazement. 'Children! What *have* you got? What in the world is all this?' they cried.

'It's the things that were stolen from that old man's house at the bottom of John's garden,' panted Sam.

The children put them all down on the floor and stood beaming at the two astonished grown-ups. 'But children, these are very, very valuable. They're the old man's treasures!' said Sam's mother, picking up the clock. 'And listen, there's a big reward offered for anyone who finds them. A – very – big – reward – and you'll get it between you, bless you. Well, well, what excitement! It's like the Fabulous Four all over again!'

'But there's only three of us,' said Rosie. 'Poor Sarah's ill in bed.'

Blackie barked, as if to say, 'No there aren't only three of you! There's me as well, and that makes four!'

Sam's and Rosie's mother laughed. 'As I said,' she smiled, 'you're the Fabulous Four all over again!'

12

A very happy ending

The next few days were really very exciting indeed. Sarah, who was getting better, was allowed downstairs in the afternoons. One day after school John took her down to the hidey hole. The others came too, and they shared some blackcurrant juice and chocolate biscuits.

'This is wonderful,' said Sarah, her eyes shining. 'Now I feel as if I belong to this adventure too!'

The police came to Sam's house, of course, and examined all the things the children had found in their hidey hole. They had a list with them, and ticked the things off one by one.

'There's a reward of three hundred pounds,' said one of the policemen. 'I should reckon that it'll be split into three as these three children found the goods.'

'Oh, brilliant!' said all three children at once.

'Now we can give it all to Miss Allen and she can put it towards the new Dogs' and Cats' Home!' shouted John.

'Don't *you* want any of the reward?' asked one of the policemen in surprise, looking at the three children.

'Well, if there's any left, we might be able to buy Blackie some bones,' said John, patting the puppy. 'He helped too.'

'Oh, we'll see that Blackie gets his bones, and I shouldn't be surprised if there's something for each of you kids too,' said the policeman, smiling. 'I'd like to see this hidey hole of yours. It sounds a useful thing to have.'

So down the garden they all went. The police didn't much like scrabbling under the blackberry bushes, but they managed to peep into the hidey hole. 'A very fine hidey hole indeed,' said one. 'A good thing you found it. If you hadn't, those thieves would have hidden their goods here in safety until they could fetch them and sell them. It was a very clever place to hide the stolen goods. No one would ever think of looking down here!'

'Hey! Hey! Hey! What are you all doing down in my garden?' cried a very angry voice suddenly. And there was the cross old man in his wheelchair, waving his stick at them. How surprised he was to see so many children *and* two policemen in his garden.

'Good morning, sir,' said one policeman politely. 'We were just on our way round to your house to tell you some good news. These children here found most of your stolen belongings hidden in this hole, and we've got them all at their house, ready for you.'

'Well, well, well! What wonderful news!' said the old man, beaming all over his face and quite forgetting to be cross. 'But what about the thieves? I hope you've caught them!'

'Not yet, sir, but we shall,' said the policeman, smiling. 'They don't know that these children found the stolen goods and they'll come to fetch them, no doubt of that. And when they come stealing back in the night and slide down into the hidey hole, they'll find something else instead of the things they stole. They'll find several strong policemen waiting for them, hidden in amongst all these black-berry bushes. Oh yes! Those thieves will be caught all right, sir!'

That night the children lay in bed and won-dered if the police were hiding down at the bottom of John's garden, waiting for the thieves. Sure enough, next day, the police called round to tell them that two men had been arrested at the hidey hole the night before. What an exciting time this was! The children had handed over to the police everything they'd found in the hidey hole, including the silver pencil, the cup, the newspaper, the keys and the knife. How delighted the police were.

'Look at this!' said one, handing the news-paper to another. 'See that name written at the top? Well, that's where the paper was deliv-ered. That's the address of one of the men. And look at the initials on the pencil: P. L. M. It looks as if it might belong to that fellow who came out of prison last month, Peter Leslie Marlow. And as for these keys, they must be the ones stolen last month, when the thieves got into Colonel John's house by unlocking the front door. They fit the description of his keys exactly. He'll be glad to have them back!'

'How amazing that the silver pencil I found is helping the police,' said John. 'I think that when I grow up I'll be a policeman. It must be a very exciting life!'

'Well, it seems to me that you children have had an exciting time too,' said the big policeman with a smile. 'Now, we'll be going. We'll see that you get your reward safely. Goodbye and good luck!'

The reward arrived the very next day, addressed to John. He gave the cheque proudly to his father. 'Will you change it into money for us, please, and as soon as you can? We want to give it to Miss Allen. She said yesterday in assembly that the school has raised just over seven hundred pounds so far. So when we give her the reward money that'll make just over a thousand pounds!'

'Splendid!' said his father. 'I'm proud of you all. Now don't forget to take a little bit of the reward for Blackie. I think he could do with a new collar as well as a good supply of bones.'

'Wuff!' said Blackie at once, wagging his tail very fast indeed.

How I wish you could see Blackie with his lovely new collar, *and* the old farm barn that was set to become the Dogs' and Cats' Rescue Home in the next village. And what did the three children have? Well, the police gave them a fine whistle each, and an extra one for Sarah, just like a police whistle, but smaller.

'To blow when you find any more mysteries that need our help!' said the big policeman who presented the whistles to the delighted children. 'Or to lend to your sports teacher at football or netball games. They'd be glad of them, I'm sure!'

They certainly are fine whistles. I hear them being blown very loudly indeed when any of the four wants to meet the others down in that exciting hidey hole. Every time I hear it I think, 'How amazing! Have the Fabulous Four found another mystery to solve?' If they have, I must certainly put it into another story for you!

Four in a Family

John and Sarah's Dad is in hospital, and they'd love to take him some presents. The only problem is that they don't have any money!

Together with their cousins, Sam and Rosie, they begin to make plans. The Fabulous Four are full of ideas about how they can earn some money, but will they really manage it? And what is Rosie's big secret for earning the most?

The Birthday Kitten

Sam and Rosie's birthdays are coming up soon, and what they've always wanted is a puppy or a kitten. But their Mum wants them to wait.

Before their big birthday party, Sam and Rosie go down to the pond to play with Sam's new sailing boat. While there, they hear a splash and see a bag in the water with something moving in it. To their surprise, they discover a tiny kitten, shivering and very hungry.

Can they keep him without Mummy and Daddy knowing? How will they nurse him back to life? And who would want to throw him in the pond?

The Very Big Secret

Sam and Rosie's Mum has had to go away for a few days and has promised to bring them back a wonderful present.

In the meantime, the two of them decide to go down to the meadows and search for honeysuckle by the stream. But when they come back, Rosie finds something incredible. What has she found? And how on earth did it get there?

Read on to see how Rosie and Sam solve their dilemma, and what Mum's wonderful present will be.

The Four Cousins

The Fabulous Four learn about some needy children in Africa and decide to help. They all start doing jobs to earn money, but Sarah and John soon turn to reading or snoozing instead of working hard. But when they hear how much money Sam and Rosie have saved up, they try to earn their own share.

How much will the four cousins earn? And what will be their wonderful reward?